W9-AFO-843

For Sylvie
in memory of life at Earls Down Farm

Dear Daddy...

PHILIPPE DUPASQUIER

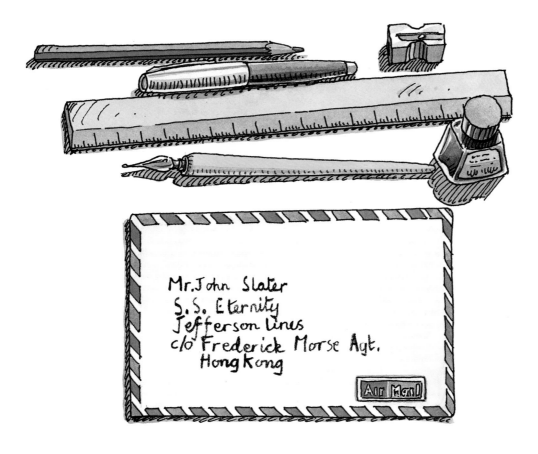

Bradbury Press/New York

Dear Daddy,
I think about you lots and lots. Are you all right on
your ship? We all miss you.

It's raining all the time at home, so Mommy bought me some red boots. They're great!

Mr. Green the gardener came to trim the hedge today.
Timmy's got a new tooth. He's got six altogether now.

Mommy says he'll soon be walking. I hope you are well. We think about you all the time.

I had a great birthday party. All my friends came, except for Jacky—she had chicken-pox. Mommy made a chocolate cake.

I had lots and lots of presents. My best one was a mask for looking underwater when we go to the beach.

School has started again. The garden is full of dead leaves. The teacher showed me on a big map where you are going on your ship.

She said it was a very long way. I wish you were home again.

It's very cold and Timmy is sick. Dr. Rush came and he looked in Timmy's mouth and listened to his chest with a stethoscope.

He said it's not too bad, and Mommy went to buy some medicine.

I liked the postcard you sent us. There's lots of snow here. Timmy and me made a huge snowman.

Mommy says if I'm good, Santa Claus might bring me a bicycle. That would be great!

Some men from the music shop brought back the old piano today. They have fixed it. Mommy is very happy.

She's going to teach me how to play it. Then when I'm big, I'll be a pianist and go around the world just like you.

When you come home, we'll do all sorts of things together. We can go walking in the woods, and fishing in the pond, just like we used to . . .

and at night-time, we'll look up at the sky and you can
tell me the story of the little prince who lives on a star.

It's not long till summer and I know we'll soon be all together again.

I think about you every day. Please come home quickly.

Love from Sophie

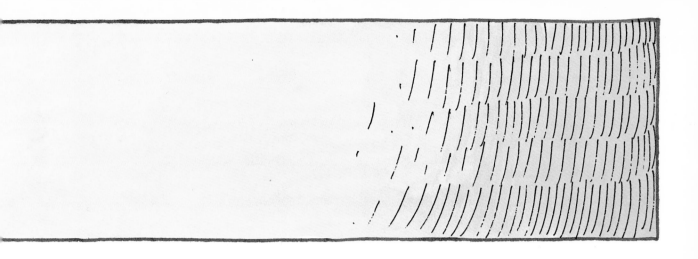

Bradbury Press
An Affiliate of Macmillan, Inc.
866 Third Avenue, New York, N.Y. 10022
Collier Macmillan Canada, Inc.

Printed in Great Britain
10 9 8 7 6 5 4 3 2 1
First published in Great Britain by Andersen Press Ltd.

Library of Congress Cataloging in Publication Data

Dupasquier, Philippe.
    Dear daddy—.

    Summary: The top portion of each double page spread
shows Sophie's father on a long sea voyage, while the
bottom portion shows her activities at home as she is
describing them in a letter.
    1. Children's stories, English. [1. Fathers and
daughters—Fiction.   2. Family life—Fiction.
3. Seafaring life—Fiction]   I. Title.
PZ7.D924De   1985   [E]   84-27505
ISBN 0-02-733170-9